WITHDRAWN

# Ghostly Tales of Route 66:
# Oklahoma to Arizona

By Connie (Corcoran) Wilson, M.S.

© Connie Wilson 2009

All rights reserved. No part of this book may be reproduced or transmitted in any form or by any means, electronic or mechanical, including photocopying, recording or by any informational storage or retrieval system, except by a reviewer who may quote brief passages in a review to be printed in a magazine or newspaper-without permission in writing from the publisher.

* * * * * * * * * *

Although the author has exhaustively researched all sources to ensure the accuracy and completeness of the information contained in this book, he assumes no responsibility for errors, inaccuracies, ommisions, or any inconsistency herein. Any slights of people or organizations are unintentional. Readers should consult an attorney or accountant for specific applications to their individual publishing ventures.

**Ghosts of Route 66: From Arkansas to Arizona** includes a worthy story from near Route 66, in Fort Smith, Arkansas, and moves on to Oklahoma, the Texas Panhandle, New Mexico and takes you to the Arizona border. For those of you brave enough to travel this road, who saw or heard things inexplicable by normal means, "Be wary of things that go bump in the night!"

At 2,448 miles long, Route 66 is more than just a road; it is Americana. Along the many stops, there are plenty of ghost stories worth retelling.

You'll get more than just your kicks on Route 66. You'll get plenty of scares, too...

**Quixote Press**
**3544 Blakslee Street**
**Wever, Iowa 52658**
**1-800-571-2665**

The reader should understand that we were able to obtain some of these stories only if we promised to obscure the actual identity of persons and/or property. This required us to occasionally use fictitious names. In such cases, the names of the people and/or the places are not to be confused with actual places or actual persons living or dead.

Quixote Press
3544 Blakslee Street
Wever, IA 52658
800-571-2665

"An unusual way of telling these tales is what sets this book apart...there is a journalistic approach, along with a recreation of them akin to an episode of Unsolved Mysteries. It's easy to see the appeal when one sees the texture they give to the stories."

("Cemetery Dance," Christopher DeRose)

## Dedication

I'd like to dedicate this book to my husband of forty-one years, Craig, who has been understanding when I wasn't available to watch a movie because I was writing, and who has listened to me read my stories aloud to him, even when he might not have felt like listening.

Also, to my wonderful children, son Scott and daughter-in-law Jessica, and their beautiful newborn one-month-old twin girls, Elise and Ava, who are just starting life. I couldn't ask for a better son and daughter-in-law and the girls, my first (and only) granddaughters, are gorgeous.

And last, but certainly not least, to my spirited daughter Stacey, who is more like her mother than she cares to admit and who makes me proud every day. I love you all with all my heart!

**Connie (Corcoran) Wilson, M.S.**

# TABLE OF CONTENTS

| | |
|---|---|
| **Cherokee Bill and the Hanging Judge of Fort Smith, Arkansas** | 19 |
| **Background of Oklahoma Route 66** | 31 |
| **Fort El Reno: Communing with the Spirits** | 42 |
| **The Buffalo Soldier of Fort El Reno, Oklahoma** | 55 |
| **The Mysterious Major of Fort El Reno** | 71 |
| **The Strychnine Specter of Fort El Reno, Oklahoma** | 81 |
| **Texas Information** | 87 |
| **The Angel Ghost Child of McLean, Texas** | 93 |
| **The Tradewinds Love Triangle** | 109 |
| **Cadillac Ranch Information** | 117 |
| **Cadillac Crazy** | 121 |
| **New Mexico: Land of Enchantment** | 132 |
| **The Tale of Tocom, Kari and Tonopah** | 135 |

## THE MOTHER ROAD

Connie points out the location of the Clinton, Oklahoma Museum on the Route 66 Map.

## The Mother Road

The Mother Road has taken many paths, beginning with the Fort Smith to Amarillo Airline Highway, the Fort Smith to California Road, the Kansas City to Oklahoma City Highway, the Ozark Trail, the Pontiac Trail, and culminating in Route 66.

One of many period photos of a Route 66 Main Street (*Note vintage cars).

**Tales of the Mother Road**

Before there was a Route 66, there was the Forth Smith to California Road, which included the Fort Smith to Amarillo Airline Highway.

Then, there was the Kansas City to Oklahoma City Highway.

Then came the Ozark Trail and the Pontiac Trail.

Next came Route 66, and, today, Interstate 40, which today's nostalgic traveler will depart from to search out vestiges of the towns and sights of the original Mother Road.

We start off with a ghost story from Fort Smith, Arkansas, site of the California Road.

I hope you enjoy it.

Author Connie (Corcoran) Wilson poses next to one of the bronze chairs, inscribed with the name of one of the victims of the Oklahoma City bombing, in Oklahoma City, Oklahoma.

## Cherokee Bill and the Hanging Judge of Fort Smith, Arkansas

Judge Isaac Parker, the hanging judge, ruled with an iron fist for twenty-one years over the western district of Arkansas, handling 13,490 cases. Today, this territory forms part of Oklahoma. Judge Parker took over the court in Indian Territory just four days after the Civil War broke out, in April of 1861. A supporter of Abraham Lincoln who felt that women deserved more rights, Judge Parker, however, was quite upset that fully two-thirds of the capital offenses he found guilty in his small courtroom were eventually overturned by the Supreme Court.

This may have contributed to Judge Parker's tendency to pronounce tough harsh sentences. Judge Parker's death sentences became so common that he earned the nickname, "the Hanging Judge," and some say he was the basis for John Wayne's character of Rooster Cogburn in "True Grit."

One fine March day in 1865, Judge Parker was sitting in his small, dark courtroom, presiding over a case against Cherokee Bill. Cherokee Bill had tried to escape from custody and, in the process, had killed one of Judge Parker's finest deputies, Zeke Payne.

Being killed in the line of duty was an occupational hazard for Judge Parker's deputies. One hundred and nine of Judge Parker's deputies were killed in the line of duty.

As Judge Parker took his seat behind the court bar, he reached for a glass of water kept nearby, took a sip, and raised his bushy white eyebrows to glare in the direction of the defendant.

"How do you plead, Bill?" Parker asked the half-breed Cherokee Indian standing before him, a prisoner who had unsuccessfully tried to escape from the long arm of the law. Bill had tried to escape twice within the past month. On the second occasion, things had gone badly and Zeke Payne, Judge Parker's deputy, had fallen backwards, breaking his neck against the cell bars of the neighboring cell during the scuffle.

Cherokee Bill stood there silently in the prisoner's docket. He chose not to respond to Judge Parker's question. Bill's buckskin jacket was dirty and his moccasins made him appear more Indian than Caucasian this day.

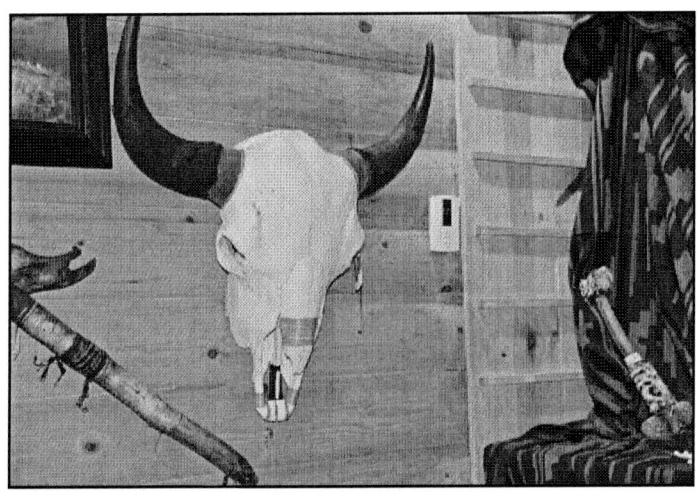

"Did you kill Deputy Zeke Payne while trying to escape from my jail on March 1st?" Judge Parker asked the prisoner in the dock for a second time.

Everyone in the courtroom knew the answer, but the question still had to be asked. Still Cherokee Bill would not respond. He spat a stream of tobacco juice towards the spittoon on the floor near the court's main bar, missing and leaving a brown stain on the weathered wooden floor of the courtroom. Judge Parker frowned. Bill's attitude and silence made Judge Parker even more irritated.

The Judge took another sip of the water in his glass. Some said the glass was filled with straight vodka. Isaac Parker denied it.

"You know my motto, Bill. 'Permit no innocent man to be punished, but let no guilty man escape.' You were a guilty man when you were brought in here, Bill…guilty of horse theft. But you weren't guilty of murder then. You hadn't killed one of my men at that point. Two days ago, when you killed Zeke Payne while trying to escape, you became a murderer and I let no guilty man escape. Zeke was just doing his job, but you took his life. He was your jailer; now he's your victim. Zeke left behind a wife and two little boys. Now, I'm going to take your life, just like you took Zeke's. I sentence you to hang by your neck until dead, Bill. I've sentenced 159 others to the same fate, and none were caught as dead to rights as you were." Judge Parker paused, took another sip of the clear fluid in his large blue glass, cleared his throat. He asked Bill, "What do you have to say for yourself?"

Cherokee Bill just squinted defiantly at Judge Parker. Once again, he aimed a stream of tobacco juice at the nearby spittoon. Once again, he missed.

Judge Parker was not about to have his sentence reversed by the Supreme Court, as had been happening with increasing frequency, much to his chagrin. Only seventy-nine of the one hundred and sixty people on whom he had imposed the death penalty had actually been executed. Judge Parker was determined that Cherokee Bill would not walk away from this charge. Cherokee Bill would not go free after killing Zeke Payne, one of Isaac's best deputies. That much was certain in the Judge's mind, and in the minds of all Judge Parker's deputies. Bill must be punished.

Judge Parker continued immediately. There was no waiting around for days to pass before sentence was pronounced. Justice was swift and sure in the Hanging Judge's court.

"I sentence you, Crawford Goldsby, to hang by your neck until dead on March 17, 1896."

The use of Cherokee Bill's given Christian name rang loudly in the courtroom. It caused more than a few raised eyebrows amongst those who had only ever known the defendant by his nickname, Cherokee Bill.

Judge Parker continued, "If you have anything to say for yourself, Bill, say it now." The Judge, like the rest of the courtroom, had returned to using the nickname by which the town knew the defendant

Cherokee Bill remained silent. He was illiterate, but he was a tough customer. Hearing the death sentence pronounced, his eyes narrowed. They were mere slits, staring at the Judge who intended to end his life. At first, that was his only reaction. Bill felt it was an Indian's duty to attempt to escape. Men were not meant to be kept penned up in cages like wild horses. Certainly men with the noble blood of Geronimo and other great chiefs of the plains were not meant to be incarcerated against their will, merely because they tried to secure a horse, as Bill had done. Bill was one angry halfbreed Indian, and he was not going to go gently into that good night.

Cherokee Bill finally replied.

"I curse you, Isaac Parker. If you carry out this sentence on me, I'll haunt you. I'll haunt your courtroom. I'll haunt your family. I'll haunt this whole godforsaken town until hell won't have it. Mark my words, you haven't seen the last of Cherokee Bill."

There was a sharp intake of breath amongst some of the womenfolk who had gathered in Judge Parker's courtroom that day to learn what was to become of the man who had killed Zeke Payne while trying to escape from Judge Parker's jail.

Six weeks later, on March 17, 1896, Cherokee Bill was led up the ten steps to the gallows, which had been constructed outside the courtroom. The execution was to take place in front of a crowd of roughly two hundred people, including two official witnesses--- people who regularly assembled to watch the spectacle of a man (or a woman, in four memorable cases) dropping to his (or her) death, feet twitching, tongue protruding, eyes bulging from hollow sockets. At the last hanging, a double hanging, one of the official witnesses, a sheriff from the nearby Oklahoma Territory, had immediately run towards a nearby juniper tree and vomited. The stench of the executed men evacuating their bowels reached past the first row of the crowd, and the entire spectacle was just too much for the gentle family man from near Fort El Reno.

Just before Bill dropped through the trapdoor to his death, Cherokee Bill repeated his vow: 'I'll haunt this town. I'll haunt this gallows. You'll never be rid of Cherokee Bill."

Cherokee Bill's body was buried in the potter's field set aside for the indigent. His grave had no marker. There were no mourners when the pine box containing Bill's earthly remains was lowered into its grave. There were no flowers.

Less than a week later, an observer passing the gallows on a windless day watched the gallows nooses swinging as though in a gale-force wind, even though there was no breeze at all that day.

Inside Judge Parker's courtroom, the pitcher of water (or was it vodka?) was always filled before Judge Parker entered the courtroom, but, on more than one occasion, a glass of the clear liquid had been poured before anyone entered the courtroom. Who had poured this glass of clear liquid? The courtroom had been locked until moments before court convened.

Cherokee Bill's presence was felt in other ways. The paperwork on Judge Parker's desk, neatly stacked by the court bailiff for the Judge's entrance into the courtroom, suddenly flew in all directions, even though there was no wind and no one was near the pile of papers. A low whistling sound could sometimes be heard, and the tell-tale stain of tobacco, aimed towards a nearby spittoon, stained the floorboards of the small, dark wood courtroom, even though no one else had been in the room and Judge Parker, himself, did not use tobacco.

The townsfolk whispered amongst themselves about the swinging nooses, the swirling papers, and the already-poured liquid in the Judge's water glass.

Things were just as haunted at Judge Parker's house. Lights turned themselves on and off. Tobacco stains were found on the carpeting. The sound of footsteps on the roof awakened those inside the house at all hours as they tried to sleep.

Cherokee Bill was right; he would never totally leave the hanging Judge's courtroom or his home.

It seems indisputable: the ghost of Cherokee Bill still haunts at least one courtroom and one home in Fort Smith, Arkansas.

**Oklahoma City Memorial**

## OKLAHOMA

Oklahoma, next door to Fort Smith, Arkansas, deserves a closer look. More of Route 66 runs through the state of Oklahoma than through any other state.

This was not accidental. Oklahoma Highway Commissioner Cyrus Avery had a national reputation among transportation officials. In 1924, he was recruited by the U.S. Bureau of Public Roads to help develop the new interstate highway system. He accepted the post and worked throughout 1925, attempting to connect hundreds of existing roads and highways to create a nationwide network for travel.

Avery was given broad authority. He wanted to make sure that one of the chosen routes would cut directly across his home state. In order to make that happen, he had to have the backing of officials in Missouri and Illinois to let the route go across Oklahoma on its way from Chicago to Los Angeles. Avery knew that the road would bring commerce to his home state, and he was not about to lose out on that opportunity.

After Avery secured the approval of the officials in Illinois and Missouri, there still remained the question of numbering the route. Avery wanted to name the new road Route 60. Unfortunately, the state of Kentucky had demanded that more prestigious zero-ending number for a route that was to cross that state, a road tentatively designated as US 62.

The argument became even more complicated, as Kentucky officials maintained that the Kentucky highway, which started in Newport News, Virginia, should connect with Avery's route in Springfield, Missouri, and create a true east-west trans-coastal highway, which would be called US 60.

This was not something that Avery wanted to agree to. It would break up his route and leave the stretch connecting Springfield with Chicago demoted to branch status. A debate raged well into the year 1926. Avery realized that he had to reach a settlement quickly, in order to have his highway project commissioned before upcoming elections jeopardized its approval.

About that time, Avery's chief engineer, a man named John Page, discovered quite by accident that the number 66 was available. Avery liked the sound of the double sixes, just as Bobby Troup's wife later liked the rhyming sound of "Get your kicks on Route 66" and suggested it to Troup for his famous song.

With all parties satisfied, Washington granted final approval to Route 66 and it was officially designated on November 11, 1926. To help promote the highway, Avery organized the U.S. 66 Highway Association just before he left office. Through his efforts, Route 66 soon became known as America's premiere highway.

The Depression soon hit, and Route 66 became a main thoroughfare for those seeking to escape the Dust Bowl states, leaving Oklahoma, Texas and Arkansas to travel to California. This entire saga was immortalized in John Steinbeck's classic novel *The Grapes of Wrath*, which dubbed Route 66, "the mother road, the road of flight."

During World War II, Route 66 became a military conduit. The continuous convoys kept the highway and the merchants busy, although Route 66, itself, paid a price, as the road was designed for civilian travel and now was suffering wear and tear from all the military usage.

This gradual decaying of the route was noticed in Washington, where discussions were already ongoing to develop a wider, faster, limited-access highway system that could handle the toughest demands of the country as it moved forward.

By war's end (1945) the damage to the infrastructure of the route had been done. The demise of the road was seen as inevitable. It would cost too much money to reinvigorate Route 66. Bobby Troup remembers the day the route was decommissioned and people were celebrating. Troup was there and said, "Why are you celebrating?" He found the death of Route 66 a sad thing, not a happy one.

However, with the war over and a return to peace and prosperity, plus Bobby Troup's jazzy hit song "Get Your Kicks on Route 66," came a new appreciation for the ability to travel this road that represented the mainstream road for America. G.I.'s home from the war who wanted to travel. The highway cashed in. Businesses multiplied along the route. Tourist traps and curio shops and an explosion of neon signs lighted the way on Route 66 with Vegas-like color. Motor courts became known as "motels," a new concept in American travel and cafes became "restaurants." General stores were dubbed "trading posts." Billboards and Burma Shave signs helped spread the word along the highway.

Over the next fifteen years, Route 66 changed substantially. It was ripped up. It was downgraded. It was shoved aside. It was realigned. Dozens of towns dependent on Route 66 traffic were suffering from the effects of all this change to the route.

The end of the 1960s, with the Eisenhower-era Interstate system moving full bore ahead, did the permanent damage to Route 66. America's Main Street had ceased to become a "through" route. It was no longer the "mother road" of Steinbeck's novel. It was now a fragmented series of pieces of the road, local highways, old motels that began to die as the tourist trade stopped, leaving interesting memorabilia that, today, local Route 66 associations seek to preserve.

Today, Route 66 is making a comeback as a road with a place in history, "the highway that's the best," the place to "get your kicks." Motorcyclists and old car enthusiasts routinely travel the Mother Road.

Lou Mitchell's Restaurant at 565 W. Jackson Blvd. is the beginning of Route 66 in Chicago, Illinois, and has been a registered historical monument since 2006.

Visitors from many foreign countries are also intrigued by the history that the old route represents, and numerous Route 66 Museums have sprung up to satisfy the new-found interest in this unique piece of Americana.

We pick up the route for the next story just outside of Oklahoma City, thirty miles west of Oklahoma City and four miles west of the town of El Reno, at the 7,000 acre Fort El Reno that is now a grazing lands research center for the United States government, but has a long and proud history that we will learn about in three stories: "The Buffalo Soldier Ghost of Fort El Reno, Oklahoma;" "The Strychnine Specter of Fort El Reno" and "The Mysterious Major of Fort El Reno."

All of these tales were stories I heard on the November 15, 2008 Fort El Reno Ghost Tour. I shot a picture with my Nikon D90 that is not able to be explained during that tour, and I was tapped on the shoulder three times by someone (or something?) who, to this day, remains unknown and mysterious.

Did the ghosts know that there was a writer present who wanted to memorialize their stories? It was the first time that something "weird" had happened to me while writing ghostly tales.

And my encounter...if it was an encounter...with those from beyond the grave is absolutely true.

**Milk bottle building icon** of Route 66 in Oklahoma City. The building now houses a business selling Vietnamese food and is a convenience store, but it has had many incarnations since being established along Route 66 as an icon of the road.

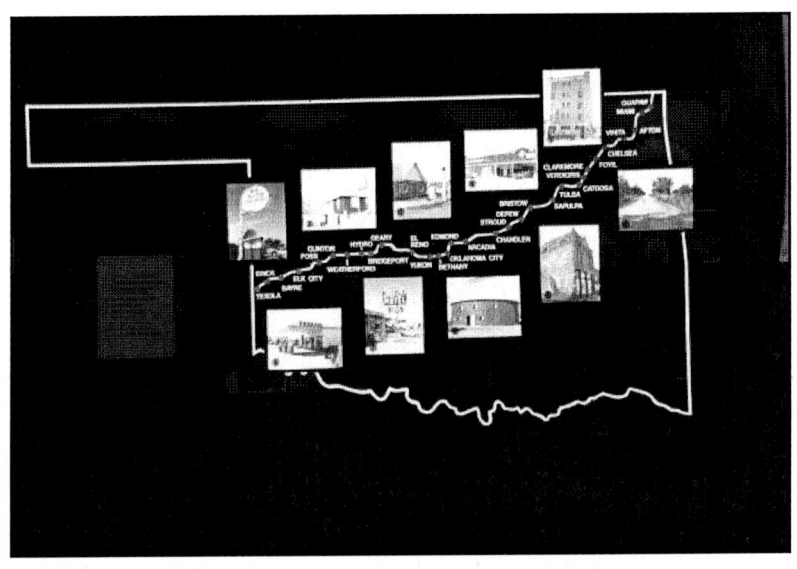

**Map showing early roads, Route 66 route.**

# Fort El Reno, Oklahoma: November 15 (2008) Ghost Tour Communing with the Spirits

When I spoke at the First Annual Route 66 Festival at the Old Chain of Rocks Bridge in St. Louis on October 4, 2008, I was asked this question: "You've been researching ghosts along Route 66 for your book *Ghostly Tales of Route 66* for almost two years now. You've already written one volume of ghost stories. Have you ever had an encounter with a ghost yourself, firsthand?"

I had to admit, somewhat sheepishly, that I had never had a ghostly encounter.

It's not that I don't believe in ghosts. I'm open to the possibility that the spirits of the deceased linger in a place and attempt to contact the living after death. I just had not heard or seen or experienced anything "ghostly"---until November 15, 2008 during the Fort El Reno Ghost Tour in Oklahoma.

Fort El Reno is about twenty miles west of Oklahoma City just off Interstate 40. It was established during the Cheyenne uprising of 1874. The post was named in honor of Major General Jesse L. Reno and served as a remount depot for the military from 1908 until 1947. The men stationed there helped escort cattle drives and served as wardens of 1,335 imprisoned World War II German POWs (part of Rommel's forces in North Africa) and helped to police the area during the Indian Wars. The riderless horse, Black Jack, used at JFK's funeral was born and raised at the Fort El Reno Today, there are no horses.

The facility today is a grazing lands research laboratory owned and operated by the U.S. government.

**USDA Headquarters at Fort El Reno.**

The ghost tour at Fort El Reno has become so popular, attracting paranormal investigators (this night, they were present with their equipment) as well as ordinary folk and devoted ghost enthusiasts that the tours, run by Bob Warren and Jessica Wells, have had to divide up the eighty or more people who routinely show up. The tour members are divided into groups of four and each group is assigned their own guide to make the five-hour walk by lantern lamplight.

This tour was added to the season schedule on November 15th because all the others were full. The tours will resume again in March. There is usually a waiting list for people to take the tour, which currently costs $6 and takes about four to five hours.

**On the grounds of Fort El Reno, Oklahoma.**

It was bitterly cold this night. I was wearing a winter coat, gloves, and earmuffs. I was ready. My husband had on only a light jacket and would end up in the car with the heater running by the time we came to the end of the tour and traveled to the old, haunted cemetery a mile away from the Visitors' Center, down a winding gravel road. He missed one of the most truly frightening set of stories about Fort El Reno, delivered by the light of the full moon in the creepy cemetery atmosphere.

**Author Connie Wilson (center) with Visitors' Center Directors Bob Warren and Jessica Wells.**

However, I wasn't ready to be personally "touched" by a ghost, nor to take a picture through the window of one of the haunted houses on the Fort's grounds that was so unusual, cloudy and filled with orbs (when all other photos I took that night were completely clear.)

# GHOSTS?

**Note the "orbs" at the bottom right of the photo.**

We gathered on the lawn outside the Visitors' Center, which was built in 1936 and renovated in 2005 after the first building burned down. We shivered in the crisp darkness as the moon rose high above the chapel, a chapel built by thirty-five World War II prisoners who had been taken captive in North Africa and were subsequently imprisoned here. The prisoners worked for eighty cents a day on neighboring farms and built the chapel to thank their captors.

The chief guide, Jessica Wells, asked each of us to select a lantern and then enter the Visitors' Center (formerly the Commandant's Quarters) to be divided into tour groups.

It was inside this house, in the green-tiled bathroom, that Major Konat committed suicide in the 1930's after his wife left him. The Major's spirit supposedly still roams the house, his medals rustling, his presence felt on the staircase landing where motion detectors are set off at 3:00 a.m. in the locked facility. The Major changes television stations from soap operas to game shows, the employees say, and they hear his heavy boots thudding across the floorboards upstairs when they are completely alone in the building. Lights go on and off after the facility is locked for the night. Water turns itself on and off in sinks. And there are coldspots. All of these things signal a ghostly presence.

Was it the ghost of Major Konat that tapped me on the right shoulder three times as I entered the building? I had turned and stepped up the one step to enter the building where we would be broken down from one large group of eighty to four smaller groups of twenty. I turned, expecting my husband to be the person who had tapped me on the shoulder. He was fifty yards away on the other side of the lawn. I looked around at the others gathered this cold fall night. Did one of them have a question for the lady who wrote the ghost stories? No one said anything. No one looked at me. We entered the building.

**Haunted Landing inside Fort El Reno Visitors' Center.**

As we were briefed on the path we would take this night, a picture fell from the wall. No one was near it. Jessica seemed unfazed, "That happens sometimes, " she said.

Jessica asked if we had any questions. I raised my hand.

"Did any of you tap me on my right shoulder three times as we were entering the building?" Silence.

"Anyone?"

No response. This was growing "curiouser and curiouser," to use the term from *Alice in Wonderland*

We left the building and walked twenty yards to the first house to the left of the Visitors' Center, a house that is supposed to be among the most haunted of all those on the grounds of Fort El Reno.

"You can't go inside the house any more," said Jessica's husband, Joe, who was leading my group. "The floors are unsafe. You can take pictures through the windows of the house, if you want.

There's still furniture inside, but it's often moved around, even though no one is allowed inside the building." He simply shrugged when asked to explain.

I took a few shots with my brand-new digital Nikon D90 through the window of the ratty old white house.

**The most haunted house on the Fort El Reno Grounds, according to tour guides.**

"Oh my God!" said the paranormal investigators present that night, upon viewing my photo. "Look at that orb in the bottom of the photo! It looks like there's a woman standing there in a bikini, with her hand on her hip." There was nervous laughter. Even more mysteriously, the picture wouldn't come up on my computer to be closely viewed for a very long time, until I had my son help me with it.

Later, on the computer, the orbs and cloudiness still presented a mystery. The three taps on the right shoulder? No explanation.

The trip to the Fort El Reno Cemetery that followed the tour of the main grounds was unnerving in the midnight chill. We traveled down a gravel road lit only by moonlight, a good mile or two from the Fort itself. We could see our breath in the wintry chill of the small cemetery as we heard more stories of POWs who had died and been buried here. There was the story of the minister's funeral. His horse-drawn hearse was hit by lightning not once, but twice, on the way to bury him in the cold clay, killing two of the four horses. The mourners couldn't wait to get out of there!

This was the kind of place you just wanted to get away from; it was surreal, spooky, isolated. It felt unsafe. It was haunted by the memories of men like German prisoner of war, Hans Seifert who, one day before he was to be released, was killed in a fiery blaze when he accidentally set fire to himself while lighting a natural gas stove.

I still have no explanation for my experiences there.

Fort El Reno at night has a spooky, haunted feeling. It is one of those places you just want to flee.

My experiences at Fort El Reno with the shoulder tapping that cannot be explained and the ghostly photo did not scare me, but they certainly provide food for additional thought about the spirit world.

## The Buffalo Soldier Ghost of Fort El Reno, Oklahoma

Clark Young was a Buffalo Soldier of Company "M", of the $10^{th}$ U.S. Cavalry. He was stationed at Fort El Reno, one of many black soldiers stationed there in the $9^{th}$ and $10^{th}$ Cavalry units and the $24^{th}$ and $25^{th}$ Infantry units.

The black soldiers were called "Buffalo Soldiers" because of their coarse black hair, which reminded
the white soldiers and the Indians of the coarse hair between a buffalo's horns, in these days when bison still roamed the prairie. The Buffalo Soldiers were brave and hard-working and helped quell the Indian uprisings during the Indian Wars with the Cheyenne and the Arapahoe.

This fine spring day, when he awakened, Buffalo Soldier Clark Young spoke to Patrick Lynch of "G" company, $4^{th}$ Cavalry, a recent arrival to the Fort. Private Lynch had entered the stables to get his horse.

It was April 6, 1875, and a fine, sunny but windy day.

The alarm had just been sounded and the Buffalo Soldiers and other units stationed at the Fort were told to mount up. The Indians were attempting to flee again, an attempt to go back to their native homes in Wyoming and Montana.

"Do you think it's a false alarm, Patrick?" asked Clark.

"I reckon not," responded Pat.

Patrick didn't much fancy acting too friendly towards the African American soldiers, but here at Fort El Reno, things were slightly more democratic. A good soldier was a good soldier, and Clark Young was a good soldier. The cemetery west of the Fort had just been established, with only one brave soldier gone to his eternal rest there, so far. But later arrivals would prove that there were brave soldiers at Fort El Reno no matter their race, color or creed. As the years went by, they would all be buried there, side-by-side: white or black, soldier or civilian, many Indians, an immigrant from China, Germans, Italians and Russians. Some of those interred in the cemetery would be civilians; some would be infants who were stillborn, or children who died young. And some would die violent deaths, such as Patrick Lynch would later at Turkey Run.

Clark began saddling up his horse, Chalk. He had named the horse after a famous Arapahoe Indian Scout, but the horse fit its name because it was a very pale palomino. The scout after whom Clark Young had named his horse was well respected. Chalk, the man, would not meet his maker until a full six years after Clark Young's death But today was the day that Clark Young would sustain wounds that would claim his life.

The soldiers rode out across the grasslands towards an area that was a few miles north of Fort El Reno and west of the Cheyenne and Arapahoe Agency. The breeze was brisk. Although it was April, there was a stark chill in the air.

The Indians had a twelve-hour head start on the cavalry. By the time Clark and his fellow soldiers reached the sandy area known as Sand Hills, the Indians were entrenched.

The Buffalo Soldiers were often placed in the most peril. They were used as front-line fighters, not only because they were brave, but also because they were considered to be more dependable than the white soldiers in 1875.

This day, Clark and three other mounted Buffalo Soldiers were told to flank a section of Sand Hills where many Indians already had dug in. Both the Indians and the soldiers were armed, and bullets were coming perilously close to the men and their mounts. Four horses would be killed this day. Five would be wounded.

Indians sometimes tried to flee to their native lands in Wyoming and Montana, and the soldiers would be sent to retrieve them and bring them back to Fort El Reno.

Horses were considered almost as valuable as Buffalo Soldiers at this remount station established by Agent John Miles as a military camp in 1874 and converted to a military post in February of 1876. The troops were there to help keep the Indians under control. The Indians were not usually hostile towards the white settlers in the area. Indeed, the fort was not a stockade at all, but a remount station where the Army bred horses and burros. The Chisholm Trail intersected with other paths on the fort grounds and horses were the fort's purpose with Wells Fargo wagons driving through the fort on a regular schedule. Many years later, when a riderless horse was requested, to serve in John Fitzgerald

Kennedy's funeral, that horse, "Black Jack," would be one of Fort Reno's finest.

Polo games, horse-riding contests, jumping competitions and other such events would become common over the years, with celebrities like Will Rogers and Amelia Earhart (who landed her autogiro at the Fort Reno airstrip in the 1920's) in attendance. During World War II.

**The riderless horse "Black Jack" from newspaper photos of the day, grew up at Fort El Reno.**

Lipizzan (or Lipizzaner) stallions would be quartered at the Fort Reno riding hall for a period of time.

Horses were very much the ruling culture of the fort. To lose a horse in battle was almost as big a tragedy as to lose a man.

Clark carefully considered his position. His commanding officer had given him and the four other men riding with him orders to try to get behind the Indians entrenched in the sand and advance upon them. It seemed like a suicide mission, but Clark would do his best, as he always did.

It was 3 p.m. on a sunny, windy Oklahoma day, as Clark and his four companions rode towards what would turn out to be Clark Young's death. Just moments after beginning their approach, Clark Young called out "John," Clark shouted to fellow soldier and friend John Kelly, "I'm hit! I'm hit!"

"Where you hit, Clark?" John Kelly shouted back to his comrade over the unnerving sound of the Indians and the concussions of the rifles firing.

The famous Lipizzan (some spell it Lipizzaner) Stallions were housed at Fort El Reno for a brief time to take part in an exhibition.

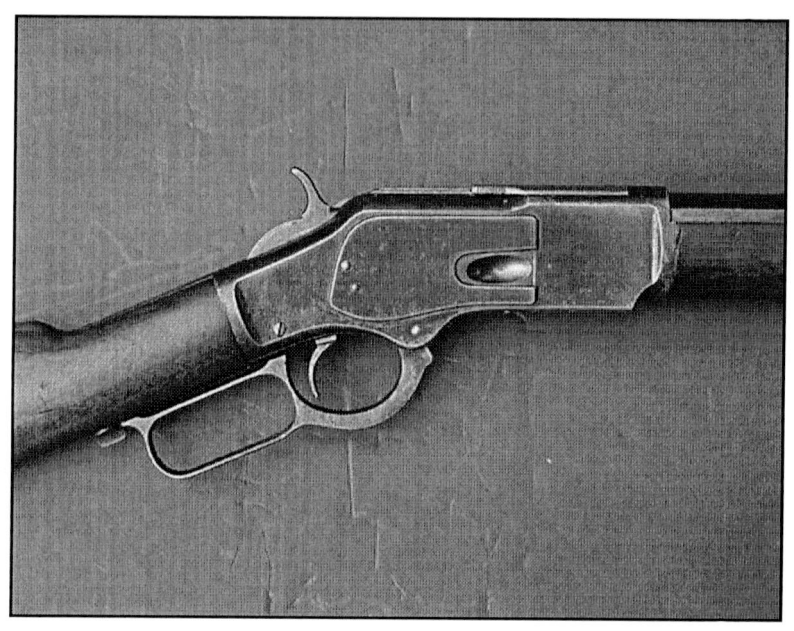

"I'm gut shot, " Clark cried back, before he fell from his mount, groaning in pain. The palomino, Chalk, stood next to his wounded master who was lying on the ground, the horse whinnying nervously and forming a temporary barrier that allowed Clark's four companions (including John Kelly) to pull him to safety. As a result of his loyalty to his longtime master, Clark's trusty mount, Chalk, was one of the four horses that sustained gunshot injuries and died in the battle that day.

The battle raged on for a good three hours, from 3 p.m. until 6 p.m. It did not end until darkness fell. The Indians fled, leaving nine dead braves behind.

Nineteen of the soldiers were wounded, but none as seriously as Clark Young. Only two others---a civilian and an Indian Scout---would die this day on the government side, but they died instantly. Not so Clark Young. He was seriously wounded, but, thanks to his trusty steed shielding his body while he lay on the ground, his companions were able to drag him back behind government lines, where it was decided that he should be taken back to Fort El Reno in one of the supply wagons.

"I'm dyin'," Clark said, between clenched teeth, to John Kelly, his best friend at the fort, as John Kelly accompanied him in the back of the wagon. Every rut in the road brought fresh searing pain to the injured Buffalo Soldier, and the road was very rutted and rugged.

"Don't talk like that, Clark. You're tougher than any other Buffalo soldier. Hang in there. We're takin' you back to the fort. The doc will fix you up."

John Kelly knew that Clark's wound was severe. As soon as John applied pressure to the gaping wound, the rags he was using to staunch the flow of blood would instantly turn red. Clark Young's intestines were clearly visible, bulging from the gaping hole and his intestines were held in only by the pressure of the two men's hands. A gut-shot soldier who sustained a wound this severe to the bowels rarely lived to see morning.

But Clark Young did live to see the morning of April 7th. He was still alive on April $8^{th}$, when most of his companions who had, by then, returned to the fort for reinforcements and supplies, left, chasing the fleeing Indians of Sands Hill. John Kelly would stay behind just long enough to see to his injured friend.

Kelly came to the bedside of his injured fellow Buffalo Soldier.

"Clark, is there anyone you want me to notify...anything you want me to do?" John and Clark had been close. They had shot wild turkeys together and been in the service of the government now as close friends and colleagues for a good two years. When they had leave, they would go into the town of 16,000 and get liquored up together. Clark had even saved John's life once, when Clark was sober but John was not.

John had begun shooting up the town. Clark had stopped him and that had probably kept John from being killed by the local Sheriff, as Alex Watkins had been, when he came back to the fort bar, drunk and disorderly, at five o'clock in the morning, and demanded entry to the closed establishment. The fort bartender had shot Alex Watkins in self-defense. But Clark Young, always a quiet, strong serious sort, had remained sober and saved John Kelly's life the night that John drank too much. Clark took charge, hustling him from the small town's streets, urging him to accompany him back to the fort. John could still hear him.

"John! John! You don't want to go getting yourself shot over a drink! Let's get the hell out of here." And with Clark at his side and guiding his horse, the inebriated John Kelly and Clark Young had made their way back to the fort and safety.

Clark was drifting in and out of consciousness, but he still knew his friend's voice. He was obviously suffering terribly. Clark could be given no water. It would be murder to give a gut-shot man water.

"John....John....I want just one thing from you before you go. Give me a drink of water."

Both men knew the significance of that request. John slowly looked into the suffering, glazed eyes of his gut-shot friend and fellow soldier, grasped his hand and asked, "Are you sure you want me to do that?"

"Yes, John. Please. Help me. Get me a drink of water."

John returned, holding a flagon of ice-cold water. It was April 12, 1875. It had been six days...six long agony-filled days of suffering for Clark Young.

John's eyes teared up as he helped the badly injured man lift his head enough to sip the ice-cold well water.

"Thank you, John. You were always a good friend."

"And you were my best friend, Clark. Had it not been for you, I would have been shot that night I got so drunk. I would be buried in the cemetery right now, if it hadn't been for you, my brother. When I am buried there, John, have them put a wire fence around my grave. Tell my mother in Stillwater where I am buried. Tell her I always loved her. You were my true friend, John. Thank you."

With those final dying words, Clark Young breathed his last, six days after the Battle of Sand Hill. Clark Young was the second person to be buried in the new cemetery at Fort El Reno, one mile down a winding gravel road from the Commander's house, with large shade trees surrounding the area set aside to bury the fort's dead.

Many would follow, of all colors and sexes, including many children. Much later, seventy World War II prisoners of war captured in North Africa, where they had served under Rommel "the Desert Fox," would be held prisoner at the fort, and thirty-five of them would also be buried here. The prisoners had been moved to Oklahoma from other locations to be held until the war ended. They worked, each day, for eighty cents on the farms of various farmers in the area. The prisoners even built a chapel to thank their captors for such good treatment.

Buffalo Soldier Clark Young of Company "M", $10^{th}$ U.S. Cavalry, died at Sand Hills while fighting bravely and his palomino horse, Chalk, died trying to protect him.

On brisk nights near the cemetery, visitors say they hear a horse whinnying in fear and, sometimes, the words, "John, get me a drink of water" can be heard whispering through the tall trees. Or maybe it's just the famous Oklahoma wind that whistles down the Oklahoma plains.

**Route 66 bridge, similar to the Old Chain of Rocks Bridge in St. Louis, Missouri.**

## The Mysterious Major of Fort El Reno, Oklahoma

One of the most fascinating stories connected with the Visitors' Center on the grounds of Fort El Reno involves Major Konat, the Commandant in the

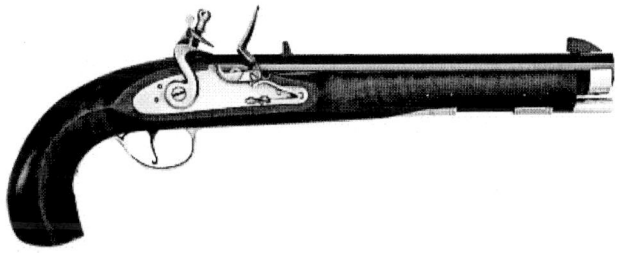

1930's. Major Konat committed suicide in the upstairs green tiled bathroom of the house.

Major Eli Konat (not his real name) was married to a beautiful woman named Lily. Lily, however, was from out East and the city of Boston. She didn't adjust well to the rural life in El Reno, Oklahoma.

Lily was a beautiful woman. Fair skin. Large blue eyes. A fetching smile. She had had many suitors in her debutante days back in Boston, but now she was married to a career Army officer. And she was stuck in rural Oklahoma, where theater and formal balls and the things she had enjoyed in her youth were not available.

Lily met a rich horse fancier at one of the frequent polo games sponsored by the fort. Will Rodgers was present at the same polo match. Amelia Earhart had piloted her autogiro, a combination airplane and helicopter, onto the airstrip at Fort El Reno for one of the polo parties in the country club atmosphere of the fort. It was not unusual to see horses and burros and all manner of grazing animal life scattered about the fort's grounds, behind fences or idling in their paddocks.

At the polo match, Lily Konat met Roger Clark. Roger had worked for the government in many foreign capitals of the world as a career diplomat. Lily and Eli were childless, which was another cross to bear. Life in Oklahoma stretched in front of her, an unendingly bleak series of grim years, interspersed only infrequently with the gaiety and merriment she had enjoyed in her days as a debutante back East.

Roger Clark, too, was smitten by the fair lovely brunette. He began making more and more frequent trips to the fort, ostensibly to observe the polo matches that attracted celebrities of the day from all over the world, but really to see Lily.

One day, Roger approached Lily with a smile.

"What's a beautiful woman like you doing in the middle of an Oklahoma field?" Roger asked.

Lily laughed. "I could ask you the same question. What's a gentleman in a suitcoat doing among all these western folk?"

Lily was obviously pleased that Roger had crossed the grassy area to speak with her. She didn't have any confidantes among the women at the fort, and her husband was a taciturn sort. Roger's compliment was well received by the fair Lily.

The two began to talk. In time, they began to fall in love. It was not easy to meet, since the town was so small and small town folk talk. But there were many events scheduled during that spring and summer and fall, and Roger Clark did his best to be present at as many of Fort El Reno's events as he could.

Winter was coming on. That meant the end of the polo matches and the end of the polo matches meant the end of seeing Roger on the grounds of Fort El Reno. Lily didn't know if she could bear it. She no longer had romantic feelings for Eli. He had become a cold, remote man who never uttered endearments or compliments of any kind. In fact, Eli rarely talked at all. He worked long hours in his top floor office and seemed completely devoted to his work. It was true that Eli paid little or no attention to his beautiful brunette bride and she became increasingly lonely in her isolation. People noticed her husband's seeming indifference to Lily, but, after the couple had been unable to conceive, it was as though Lily ceased to exist for Eli. Some other women of the fort were heard to mutter that old saying, "She made her bed. Now she'll just have to lie in it."

Roger, in stark contrast to Eli, was constantly complimenting Lily on her natural beauty. He called her "my little bluebird of happiness." Roger made Lily's heart beat faster. He made life worth living. The lonely affection-starved wife would have died of loneliness and lack of affection, had it not been for Roger Clark.

But there was nowhere she and Roger could go to be alone while she was married to Eli and living at the fort. There was no way they could sneak away for even an hour to be alone, without a great deal of effort.

Finally, Roger broached the subject they had both been thinking about.

"Lily, you have to tell Eli that you are leaving him. This is no life for a beautiful woman like you. Come away with me to Boston. I have other homes in Philadelphia and New York. Your life can be like it was before. You were not born to this life."

When Lily and Roger spoke of how she had ended up married to Eli in the first place, one fact emerged: her parents had pressured her to marry someone…anyone…because she was past twenty-one and they feared she would become an old maid.

When the handsome Major from Kansas, in charge of a major U.S. government facility, met their daughter at a Washington, D.C. ball while they were both visiting in the city, Eli was smitten and proposed immediately. Against her better judgment and over her objections, her parents insisted that she accept Eli's proposal.

So it was that Lily Konat became the wife of Major Eli Konat and ended up residing on the wide-open plains of Fort El Reno in the **Commandant's Quarters.** (Pictured below)

But now, having met Roger Clark, the chance to resume her former life of luxury and parties and balls was too tempting to resist. The choice between Roger and Eli was not a difficult one, after the long dry years on the fort.

"I'll send a wagon and a driver for you tonight at 5 p.m. The train leaves at 6 p.m.. Don't be late. We'll have a wonderful life together, my little bluebird," said Roger. He kissed her affectionately on the cheek.

Lily did not have a cruel personality. She was just lonely and she had married the wrong man for the wrong reasons. She waited until the final moment to tell Eli that she was leaving.

When Lily did tell Eli, as gently as she could, he sank to his desk chair on the first floor and sat there in silence. He didn't ask Lily why. He didn't beg her to stay. He didn't argue. He just sat there, looking completely forlorn. Eli had never been good with words. He was poor at communicating and now he was becoming even less communicative as the love of his life walked out the door of the Fort El Reno Commandant's house never to return.

Most people did not realize that Lily Konat had left Eli for several days. They thought she was just off on one of her many shopping trips to nearby cities like Oklahoma City thirty miles to the east, trips that she took to relieve the excruciating boredom and monotony of life on the Oklahoma prairie.

The townsfolk realized just how depressed Eli Konat had been when they discovered his body in the tub of the green-tiled bathroom upstairs. Eli had shot himself in the head. With consideration for those who would have to clean up the mess, he had done so while lying in the tub, fully clothed in his Major's uniform. Major Konat left no note.

There are those today who say that Eli can be seen climbing the staircase to the upstairs bedrooms and bathroom, his bloody head downcast, clad in his Major's uniform. He often pauses on the staircase to gaze out the large window. He wears all his medals, which make a slightly metallic rustling noise. There are cold spots on the staircase landing, where the Major is said to pause and look morosely out over the grounds of the fort. Motion sensors in the building have been set off on the landing leading to the upstairs, even though the entire building was locked and dark. It was 3 o'clock in the morning. There are cold spots in the upstairs green, tiled bathroom, the scene of Eli Konat's suicide.

Some say the Major still roams what is now the Visitors' Center of Fort El Reno. He says nothing, which was nearly the case during life. But those below can hear his heavy footsteps on the floor above, even though they are in the building alone. Lights mysteriously turn on and off. Water faucets will begin to fill the tub when no one else is inside the old Commandant's home.

There is often a sickly sweet dead body-rotting odor. Workers in the visitors' center hear keys rattling. At 2:30 in the morning the caretaker observed the lights flickering. Then, as he stood there horrorstruck, the door to the bedroom opened slowly and the bedroom light came on before quickly being extinguished. Voices are heard, when no one is upstairs.

Once, a wedding was being held on the grounds of the fort. The bride was sent upstairs with her bridesmaids to put on her wedding dress. It was no more than ten minutes before she came downstairs, saying, "There's a man up there."

Everyone downstairs reassured the skittish bride that she and her bridal party were the only people who had been allowed to access the upstairs, but the young woman kept maintaining that there was a strange man walking about silently.

"Get him out of there," she said. "I can't change into my bridal dress until he leaves." When the caretakers of the fort's visitors center went upstairs to investigate, there was no one there, but water was running in the bathroom sink and none of the bridal party had turned it on.

Televisions in the new facility, remodeled in 2005, come on and off by themselves. Current caretakers Bob Warren and Jessica Wells say that the ghost does not like soap operas. He prefers game shows and will change the channel without notice. Water turns on and off when nobody else is present.

When Eli Konat killed himself, he was not buried in the fort's cemetery. His family took him back to Kansas to be buried in the family plot.

A gnarled figure of an old man is sometimes seen trudging uphill towards Fort El Reno, which is four miles west of the town of El Reno. He is known as the Mystery Man of Fort El Reno.

When you drive past the man, he reappears a few miles down the road.

There are those who say the mystery man of Fort El Reno is Major Eli Konat, as he attempts to make his way back to the Fort El Reno cemetery where 200 of his comrades have been buried for nearly seventy-four years. Perhaps Eli hopes that his bride, Lily, will return to him, if he can just find his way back to Fort El Reno's small cemetery.

## The Strychnine Specter of Fort El Reno, Oklahoma

The guardhouse at Fort El Reno was used for many things. Sometimes, drunk and disorderly native American Indians who had had too much to drink were imprisoned in the basement. There were stories about their poor treatment at the hands of their captors.

But one soldier, in particular, twenty-five-year-old William Stockwell, came to a bad end in the guardhouse on April 24, 1885.

William, or Bill as he was known, had been on assignment helping escort a cattle drive up from Texas to protect the cattle from Indian raids.

On the way back to the fort, Bill began to feel sick. He knew the symptoms and he knew the cure: quinine.

"I hope we make the fort before sundown," Bill said to Jack Whitfield, one of his traveling companions. "I'm feeling poorly. I need medicine."

Just then, the uphill road leading to the fort's stone entrance could be seen in the distance. Bill breathed a sigh of relief. He needed something for this pain in his stomach, and he hoped that the infirmary would be well stocked with quinine.

When they reached the fort, instead of rushing to the infirmary for medical care, Bill was seized and taken to the guardhouse.

"Why? What's the charge?" he asked. The pain was becoming more and more unbearable and he was taken completely by surprise.

"You murdered the trail boss, Henry T. Stevens, in cold blood on your last ride from Caldwell, Kansas up through Fort Worth. We heard tell that, after you set out on that ride on March 3, 1882, the third day you told the others, 'I'm tired of riding with you all today. I've had enough of you. You had better get going up over that hill.'"

The story told later was that the men had been lounging around an open campfire at the time. The speaker---and the guards were accusing Bill Stockwell--- was the only one who was armed. Most of the party was sitting around the campfire relaxing, when suddenly the only one of the group wearing six shooters told the others, "I'm sick of your company. You'd best begin high-tailing it for the woods, up over that ridge yonder."

The majority of the group, looking startled at the threat, did exactly that. However, one member of the group gathered around the campfire, Henry T. Stevens, spoke up. There was good reason for Stevens to speak his piece, as Stevens was the nominal leader of the group, the trail boss.

The speaker lounging by the campfire twirled his pair of loaded six-shooters with an ominous gleam in his eyes.

"What are you talking about, Bill? We've only been on the trail for three days. This is unconscionable. I'm the boss here!" said Stevens.

**Fort El Reno Guardhouse, today.**

These remarks did not set well with the shooter. He shot Henry Stevens in the chest, shot him dead on Sunday, March 16, 1882. That was three years earlier. It had taken some time to try to figure out who, exactly, was the guilty party.

Suspicion had pointed towards William Stockwell. Now, Bill Stockwell was being seized to stand trial, just as he was feeling his worst. And, to make matters even more unfair, he was innocent of the charge.

Into the tiny, dank, basement jail cell Bill went, despite his protestations of innocence.

"Please. I need quinine. Get me some quinine. I'm sick," Bill repeated, over and over. "Help me! Help me!"

His jailers brought Bill an unmarked blue bottle. It might be quinine, but the bottle looked remarkably like the ones that held a fatal poison, strychnine. Drugs were not that well supervised or that well marked, in those days. Even today mix-ups can occur if medicine is poorly marked.

"Are you sure that's quinine?" asked Bill. The bottle bore no markings to confirm its contents. It was blue and identical to the one that held the life-saving medicine quinine, which was used to treat malaria, but also had analgesic, pain-relieving properties, and anti-inflammatory properties and could be used for treating diseases like arthritis. If you felt poorly, had a bacterial infection or were in pain from an inflammation, quinine was the cure. It was the gift of the Peruvian Indians who discovered it, and it was the cure-all drug of choice in the 1880's.

When the bottle was brought to Bill's cell, he was uncertain about taking the medicine because it was not clearly marked as quinine.

The jailer, Fred Harvey, said, "Go ahead. Take it and quit your belly achin.'"

"How do I know it's quinine and not strychnine?" asked Bill.

At that, Fred laughed openly, put his little finger into the bottle, and gingerly tasted the contents. "See," he said. "It's quinine. Now take it. You've been griping about getting you some quinine to cure a stomach ache ever since we locked you up in the pokey, so take it and shut up."

Apparently convinced by Fred's show of tasting the medicine, Bill took the blue bottle and drank deeply.

Within moments, William Stockwell was in horrible pain. He doubled over, clutching his stomach. He fell to the floor, writhing in pain, foam coming from his mouth, wracked with convulsions.

Watching someone die from strychnine poisoning is not pretty. It took almost two hours for Bill to die, despite efforts to save the stricken man. As he lay dying in the jail cell of the Fort El Reno

Guardhouse, Bill Stockwell said, "I curse you, Fred, and all of you who have unjustly accused me of the death of Henry Stevens. You've killed me! You've not heard the last of William Stockwell."

With those dying words, Bill Stockwell passed on, but, say the keepers of the old fort, his spirit remains, haunting the ruins of the old Fort El Reno guardhouse. People who enter the guardhouse…especially the lower basement area where the cells were located…hear a man groaning in pain. They sometimes hear chains rattling. And some claim to hear a voice whispering, "Help me! Help me!"

## TEXAS: ROUTE 66

The path of Route 66 through the Texas panhandle, after you leave Oklahoma, with its Museums in Clinton and Elk City, is not a smooth one. In 1926, the road was essentially a series of fragments of what was once the mother road.

The highway was concrete and two-lane, but later much of the two-lane highway was divided into four-lane highway. Even later, the alignments that went forward were absorbed by I-40, which has usurped the role that Route 66 once played in conveying cars and trucks from one place to another.

Early stretches, which never saw paving, remain. Others have vanished. The area most noted for this is just west of McLean, Texas, where the oldest alignments were south of the I-40 service road. It reemerged in two places to crawl across ranch lands, before it slowly curled back towards the ghostly, windswept town of Glenrio, a place of prowling dogs and tumbleweed. There are few buildings left in this forgotten border town.

McLean, itself, has only the restored 1930's era Phillips 66 station and a museum exhibit dedicated to the history of barbed wire and its importance in the areas, which has been dubbed "Devils' Rope." It is located at Route 66 and Kingsley Street, at 100 S. Kingsley Street, east of downtown.

Everywhere you look, when you are present on McLean's main street, there are dilapidated old buildings, abandoned places that have fallen into disrepair. The few people who remain in this town are poor, many living below the poverty level. While the town once had a population of 1500, in 1940, today, it has shrunk to only 830 people and 1.2 square miles.

Of that number, 12.8% of families and 16.4% of the population live below the poverty level. If you are young, it is even worse, with 17.9% of those under eighteen living below poverty levels and 15.2% of those sixty-five and older struggling, according to the most recent census. It is not a thriving, prosperous town, as it once was.

The town began when Alfred Rowe, a prosperous English rancher, donated money to buy land to found the town in 1901. That very same Alfred Rowe would later drown on April 15, 1912, when the Titanic sank as he was sailing back to McLean from England. It was said that he was found frozen to death, floating on an ice floe, clutching his briefcase, with his expensive gold watch still ticking.

The town Rowe founded was named McLean after Judge William P. McLean (1836-1925), a member of the Texas Legislature and the Railroad Commission.

The railroad brought a degree of prosperity to the town early on. In fact, in 1904, McLean had three general stores, a bank, two wagon yards, a livery stable a lumberyard, and a newspaper the *McLean News*. A windmill was built to supply the town with water and, in 1909, the town was incorporated.

Route 66 brought even more prosperity to the town when it came through, and, in 1940, there were 1,500 people, six churches, fifty-nine businesses, and, two years later, a POW camp was established east/northeast of town that housed 3,000 Germans captured in north Africa from 1942 until 1945.

There are very few men left in McLean, compared to females. The ratio of women to men is 100 to eighty and, if you are under eighteen, it is worse, with 100 males to only seventy females.

It is not a town where women do well, and the ghost story I am about to relate will prove that.

## The Angel Child of McLean, Texas

Old Route 66 crosses under Interstate 40 at Exit I-46, today, and, eventually, you come to 302 North Main Street, where the McLean Library, part of the Texas Panhandle Library System, was commissioned in the 1940's by a vote of the city council. The McLean City Council dedicated ten dollars a month to establishing and maintaining a public library system for the town's 1,500 inhabitants, nearly double today's number of residents.

Mrs. Lady Bryand was hired to be the librarian. She worked noon to five in the library in 1942. Soon, she approached the city fathers, asking for help.

"Mayor Rece," said Lady, "I need another woman to help me with the books. When the prisoners came to town, my duties expanded along with the 3,000 Germans who want to use the library." Lady Bryand said this in a tone that indicated both desperation and exhaustion.

Lady Bryand was referring to the prisoners of war captured in North Africa, Rommel's troops, who had been brought to a prison area two miles north of McLean and one mile north of County Line Road to serve time at the McLean Permanent Alien Internment Camp. Some had been sent to Fort El Reno in Oklahoma. There were twenty to thirty buildings established near McLean to provide for the housing and feeding of the 3,000 prisoners, who began arriving in 1942 and would be held there until July 1, 1945, when the camp disbanded at the end of World War II.

Not only did the POWs physical needs require tending, but also many of the inmates of the Internment Camp needed mental stimulation in their dreary lives. Nearly all had learned English. They wanted to check out books from the small town library to improve their language skills and also to help pass the time. But, obviously, they could not stroll into town to pick out a book. Lady Bryand needed a helper, someone who could tend to the prison population, take them books, and help her with the local library needs of the townspeople, as well.

Those prisoners who had not yet learned English were picking it up quickly as they worked for area farmers. All were bored and lonely, far away from their families. Sometimes, prisoners would escape, but they would soon be found wandering the bleak Texas landscape. Most seemed almost grateful to be returned to the

McLean Permanent Alien Internment Camp where they could count on three square meals a day and, if Lady Bryand had her way, where they could improve their minds by reading books from the small town library, for which her new assistant would be responsible.

The city fathers approved the hiring of an assistant for Lady Bryand, and that was how Grace Dunham (not her real name) came to be selected for the post. Grace lived near Lake McClellan, twelve miles west of town. Living on the banks of the 325-acre lake that was known as the Paradise of the Panhandle had its drawbacks, but it also had its benefits.

You could throw a line in and catch black bass, crappie, blue cat, hybrid white-stripers, and catfish, but twelve miles was twelve miles and Grace's old jalopy, a Ford Model A, had seen better days. There was also the need to buy gas, at a time when gas was rationed. If Grace wanted to take this library job and keep it, she was going to need a reliable method of transportation, a way to either maintain the ancient automobile her deceased husband had left her, or to purchase and service a new car.

At first, Grace kept the old car running with the good will of her neighbors, the Greens and by the offices of the owner of the local Phillips 66 gas station, Bob Hooper. Mr. Green knew a thing or two about cars. He would help Grace out of a jam whenever her vehicle broke down, as it frequently did.

"It's your fan belt, Grace," Mr. Green said, on one such occasion. "You need a new fan belt." When Samantha visited the Phillips station next, Grace would have to talk to Bob Hooper about what that might cost.

Grace had a ten-year-old daughter Samantha, named after her dead father. Sam Dunham died at Normandy on D-Day. Samantha, his namesake, was nine years old then. She was a winsome child with light brown hair, big brown eyes, and a fetching smile. Samantha was artistically talented and enjoyed art projects of various sorts. She and her mother would work on these projects together during the lonely Texas winter nights.

Grace and Samantha would make little angel dolls out of string and take them down to McLean's main street, near the Phillips 66 station where tourists frequently filled up their cars for nineteen cents a gallon as they drove through McLean on Route 66.

The station, just two blocks west of Main Street at $1^{st}$ and Gray Streets was of the sort known as "cottage fashion." The owner, Bob Hooper, who had operated the station since it opened in 1928 as the first Texas service station for the Oklahoma-based Phillips 66 brand, would let the tiny ten-year-old sit inside the station on a wooden stool, selling angel dolls to the customers who frequented the station.

Bob knew how tough things were for Grace and Samantha, and he thought this was the least he could do to help them out.

Whenever Grace would come to him with another hard luck story about her old car, he would mysteriously find a fan belt that nobody wanted, which, according to Bob, "is just taking up space in the garage," and it would be installed in Grace's aging vehicle at no charge.

It was 1942. The small station had been in operation for fourteen years. It would operate for close to fifty years and be renovated in 1992. Since gas was nineteen cents a gallon, Samantha priced the angel dolls at nineteen cents.

"Please, Ma'am," she would say, if the person paying for the gas was female, "it's just one more gallon of gas." She would look hopefully up at the female tourists with her big brown eyes, and hope that the motoring women would take pity on her and her mother, marooned in poverty-stricken McLean, Texas.

Samantha and Grace had almost no money for anything but the barest essentials in these hard days. Her mother's job at the library as an assistant assigned especially to the nearby prison brought in just enough to keep their old Model "A" running, but not enough to keep the car running and also keep them eating. There were many nights when they both went to bed hungry if the fish weren't biting in Lake McLellan. Gas, flour, sugar: many of these things were rationed now, as the war wore on. Everything was expensive.

Sometimes, if the buyer of the gasoline was male, Samantha would put on her prettiest dress---really, her only dress--- and say, "Please, Mister, can you spare the cost of one gallon of gas for a widow whose husband died in the war? That was my daddy, Sam." More often than not, the male driver would gruffly toss a quarter into Samantha's mason fruit jar, in which she kept the money she earned from the sale of the homemade angel dolls.

Meanwhile, Grace was making twice-a-week trips to the prison nearby. She had met a POW named Rainier Kuechler. It was "verboten" (forbidden) to have a personal relationship with a POW. Both knew it, but the men who were imprisoned on the edge of McLean had a great deal of freedom to work in the fields of nearby farms (for eighty cents a day) and Rainier was sent to work on the Green's farm, very near Grace's place on Lake McLellan.

The two met and kept meeting, as Grace brought books to the men imprisoned on the edge of McLean on a regular schedule, and, in time, they fell in love. When Rainier was assigned to work in the Greens' fields, near Grace's small cottage, the two found time to steal away to the tiny slice of heaven represented by Grace's small cottage bedroom. Samantha, after all, was in school all day, and Grace was, more often than not, supposed to be handling her duties at the nearby prison.

"Rainier, do you think that we are wrong for doing this?" asked Grace, as she buttoned her blouse, preparing to drive her lover close enough to the McLean Permanent Alien Interment Camp that he might walk the rest of the way back to his barracks without attracting attention.

"What can be wrong about love, Fraulein?" asked Rainier, in his thick German accent. He was a handsome man with a thick shock of salt-and-pepper gray hair, a mustache, and a strong physique. Grace had not realized how much she missed her dead husband, until Rainier came into her life. At first, she had wondered how the handsome German had remained single for so long, but those thoughts were soon shoved aside during afternoons of stolen ecstasy.

After the two had been secretly meeting for nearly a year, while Samantha was at school, Grace was curled in Rainier's strong arms after making love. Grace said, "Rainier, I have something to tell you." A smile played about the corners of her lips as she imagined how pleased he would be to learn that they were to become the parents of a child. Rainier had often talked of his love for Grace and how he wished to marry her when he was released permanently from prison. He had said he wanted to remain in Texas, his adopted homeland, with Grace and Samantha.

"I, too, have something to tell you," said Rainier. As he did so, he pulled a wrinkled envelope from his pants pocket. He didn't look Grace in the eye as he spoke, telling her of the letter from Germany.

The two had started out not talking about the past, but only of the future. Over time, Grace had shared the story of her courtship and marriage to Sam, his death at Normandy Beach on D-Day. Rainier had described himself as an aging bachelor who welcomed the thought of a new family and a lovely stepdaughter---a "ready-made family," as he called it--- to enrich his lonely life.

Now, Rainier was about to confess that his story had all been a lie.

"My wife wrote me today," said Rainier to Grace. She was stunned.

"Wife? Your wife? But…you said that…you said that you had never married…that you loved someone who did not love you back…that you had remained single all these years."

"I know, Liebchen," said Rainier, using a German endearment, "but I lied. I didn't know you that well at first. Now, I do, and I can't go on lying to you. I have a wife and three children at home in Hamburg."

Grace felt a wave of shock wash over her, at first. Then she felt something else. She had given herself freely to Rainier. He had talked of the life they would build when his time was up at the encampment. He had told her that he had never been married. He had never once hinted at a wife and a child, let alone a wife and three children. Now, she realized, everything he had ever told her had been a lie. She was completely enraged.

The two had walked outside, so that Grace could drive Rainier close enough to the prison so that he could return from his (supposed) day in the Greens' fields. The two had been very careful to conceal their meetings. They always left through the back of the small house, away from prying eyes, back near the woodshed and the woodpile, where an axe was now stuck in a log, waiting to behead some chicken for dinner.

A wave of anger unlike anything she had ever experienced took control of Grace's emotions. As she described it later, to Samantha, "When he told me this, something inside of me died. I just snapped. I grabbed the axe and flung it at Rainier. I didn't think. I didn't talk. I just reacted."

The axe embedded itself firmly in Rainier's forehead. He dropped "like a sack of potatoes," as Grace's father used to say. Rainier was probably dead before he hit the ground. The blade of the axe had penetrated his skull and embedded itself deeply in his brain. He never saw it coming and never felt a thing. Young Samantha, hearing this story for the first time as she returned from school, was as upset as her mother. She was horrorstruck and frightened.

"What should we do? Where should we go?" the now nearly-eleven-year-old girl asked her pale and frightened mother.

"I can only think of one thing to do, " said Grace. "I cannot drag a big man like Rainier far. But I do know how to dress a deer or a bear and cook the meat." She gave her daughter a knowing look.

*****************************************************

At first, Samantha didn't understand what her mother was trying to tell her, but then she understood.

"I will do whatever I must to help you, Mother," said the young girl. And the two set out for the back yard to dismember Rainier Kuechler, bury his bones and the parts of his body that they hacked off with axe and saw, and dispose of most of his body parts by cooking and eating them.

"We must wipe up all the blood that we see in the dirt of the yard," Grace told her daughter as she removed Rainier's prison issued uniform. "But with a large animal, the throat is slit first and they are hung, upside down, to bleed out." Grace explained to her daughter that this was necessary to preserve the quality of the

meat.

The two rigged a pulley-like instrument to the gable of the small cottage, working feverishly against the time when the prison authorities would realize that Rainier had not returned from the Greens' fields and the authorities would come looking for him.

"Get some containers for the blood," Grace directed.

Samantha looked frantically in their small kitchen for bowls and cups and other receptacles. She even emptied the change from her angel mason jar and brought that to her mother, as well.

The largest bowl was filled first, as the burly German's body hung upside-down against the back of the house, his body bumping against the eaves as though he were a character from a Hansel and

Gretel fairy tale, blood flowing freely from his slit throat to the receptacles below.

When the biggest bowl in the house had been filled with blood, the two began to use other containers until, finally, Samantha's mason jar for money was the only empty container left in the back yard. Dusk would be upon them soon. They had cut Rainier's dead body down and drawn and quartered him. Grace was using all her skill as a woman of the woods to gut the giant German and to preserve the edible portions: liver, pancreas, heart, and loins.

As she cut her lover up, she muttered, again and again, "How could you! How could you?" She looked distraught and sounded incoherent. Her white apron was spattered with the blood of the man who had pledged his love to her, when another far, far away had already claimed his love.

Finally, the two had buried Rainier's head, hands, feet and innards, and divided the edible portions of Kuechler into small packages, which they wrapped in white butcher paper that they had on hand for Samantha's art projects.

"You must never tell anyone of this, Samantha," her blood-soaked and disheveled mother said. "You cannot tell a living soul."

"I won't, Mommy. You can depend on me," answered Samantha.

"Drink this, and we will take an oath," said Grace, handing Samantha the mason jar that her daughter used to collect contributions for the angel dolls she sold at the Phillips 66 station. The mason fruit jar was now filled with Rainier Kuechler's still-warm blood.

Each woman drank of the blood of Rainier Kuechler and swore an oath, one to the other.

"I will never tell anyone what has happened here today," said Samantha."

Her mother looked into her daughter's eyes. "Nor will I," said Grace.

Samantha Dunham's childhood ended that day.

Samantha still sold angel dolls to tourists at the Phillips 66 station. She was quieter and seemed sad. For a while, it seemed as though Samantha and her mother were eating better than they had in months. Physically, Samantha looked healthier, slightly chubbier when she had been as thin as a newborn baby bird, but psychologically, she seemed scarred. The pretty little girl with the angel dolls for sale was now the young woman with a secret.

To the end of her days, neither told what had happened to Rainier Kuechler that day in McLean, Texas. The prison authorities assumed Rainier had successfully fled to another state, as happened sometimes with escapees.

When alone at night near the restored Phillips 66 station, McLean townsfolk say they see a woman, who looks deranged, drinking blood from a mason jar. They think they hear her mutter, "How could you! How could you!"

They also talk of a sad little girl, who looks like an angel herself, who sometimes stares vacantly from a small window of the now-empty Phillips 66 station, looking out at the world through the panes of the small cottage-like building, never smiling, looking wistfully out at the world like a girl whose childhood ended too soon.

**Fort El Reno Mural**

## The Tradewinds Love Triangle

The couple had spent the evening dancing the night away to Tommy Dorsey's Orchestra at the Nat in Amarillo, Texas, which used to stand for natatorium, or swimming pool. The swimming pool had long since been covered over to make a dance floor. All the big bands played there in the late twenties and early thirties and flappers flocked to the joint, arrayed in their finest.

The place was called Nat's Dine & Dance Palace and was located in Amarillo (TX) on $6^{th}$ and Georgia on Route 66. It was 1928 and Tommy Dorsey had just concluded his final set of the night.

Louise adjusted her short white shimmery flapper skirt and asked her date, J.L. Tucker, for a cigarette.

"You know I don't like it when you smoke, honey," said J.L.

"Oh, come on, J.L. Don't be such an old fuddy-duddy!" Louise shimmied across the seat of the black convertible towards the driver. He sighed in mock exasperation as he took out a silver cigarette case, extended it to the lovely blonde, and lit the Fatima cigarette she removed from the pack.

"Why do you smoke when you know I hate it?" J.L. started the engine.

"I don't do it to be mean, Honey," Louise said, simultaneously inhaling and immediately afterwards coughing slightly. "I just need the buzz."

"I'll give you a buzz," said J.L. He reached over and put his hand on Louise's thigh. She just laughed. Then she began to hum, "I Get Sentimental Over You," one of Tommy Dorsey's songs. She spritzed some Chanel from a small perfume she carried.

"His trombone playing is just too good. It makes me feel all warm and sexy," said Louise. "And it's not like you're not going to kiss me because I just had a cig, is it?" She knew the answer to that one before she even asked the question.

J.L. agreed with both of Louise's statements. "Yup. He's pretty good, all right. Especially for a trombone player."

J.L. was happy to hear that Louise felt "all warm and sexy." He had some plans for her, once they reached Airport Hangar Number Twelve.

"He's got such good breath control," said Louise, exhaling an "O" circle of smoke. "I wish I had that kind of breath control."

"What do you need breath control for?" asked J.L "You don't play a musical instrument."

Louise just gave him a sideways flirtatious glance. "I might play an instrument. I might pick one up. Soon. And I might need breath control to play it well. And I'll bet that Dorsey fellow is just the man who could teach me some tricks."

She laughed a merry laugh, slightly naughty, enjoying the innuendo of her remarks.

J.L. said, "I like the sound of that!"

"You men. You only have one thing on your minds. And you married men are the worst of all!" Louise ashed her cigarette over the edge of the convertible's passenger-side door, onto the pavement of Route 66.

"Why did you bring up the fact that I'm married?" J.L. sounded like he was going to pout now.

"Oh, Sweetheart. I didn't mean anything by it. But shouldn't we be getting back to the Tradewinds Airport? We need to get you back to the little woman on time. Wouldn't do to have her angry with you. Remember last time you were late?" Louise was only half-kidding. She had heard stories of Cynthia Tucker's temper. She didn't want to run afoul of her in person. Once, J.L. had sported a three-inch gash over his right eyebrow. Cynthia had thrown an ashtray at him during an argument over his late return home from "one of your plane trips," as Cynthia called his trips to see women other than his wife. J.L. would claim he just went to hear the bands. Cynthia hated to fly and didn't like the music, the noise, the booze or the cigarette smoke, so she stayed home, fuming.

Cynthia knew that J.L. cheated on her, but she felt she didn't have much of an alternative to putting up with it. She didn't have any money of her own, and divorce was not common in 1928. Besides, if she divorced J.L. she'd have to give up the lifestyle she had become accustomed to, and that wasn't going to happen. She'd rather die.

Louise gave J.L. a sideways look, trying to see if she was pushing any buttons. She didn't want to make him really mad. He was rich, after all, and a good dancer. J.L. took her to all the best places. Just in the last month, he had taken her to hear Benny Goodman, Duke Ellington, Guy Lombardo and, now, Tommy Dorsey. They flew to a lot of nearby towns where the bands played. If she wanted to hear Satchmo, next month at the Nat, she had better mind her "P's" and "Q's." So, Louise shut up as J.L. turned the key and the engine of the convertible roared into life. It was a black convertible with a cream interior and it was a smooth ride.

The two drove towards the Tradewinds Airport on Route 66. The road, in those days, led directly through the airport, and J.L. was flooring it. He wanted to have some time alone with Louise before they had to board his private plane and take off to fly back to Glenrio, where J.L. lived with his brunette wife, Cynthia, and where Louise worked as an assistant to a local photographer.

J.L. had been married to Cynthia now for fifteen years. He was thirty-five. He was bored. Louise was just the ticket. Louise just wanted to have fun. No strings attached. Just the way J.L. liked it. Hot and sexy.

J.L. began to smile as he thought of the fun he and Louise would have inside the airport hangar in his plush convertible, before they boarded his private plane to fly home.

The winding pavement of Route 66 was leading them towards the bright lights of the airport, which were looming in the distance. J.L. was horny, and the closer they got to the Tradewinds Airport, the hornier he got.

They arrived at Hangar Twelve. J.L.'s private two-seater was inside the hangar, awaiting their return. He shut the engine down, took the nearly dead cigarette from Louise's fingers, and tossed it from the car. Then, he grabbed the pretty blonde around the waist and pulled her towards him. The white bodice of her glittery short dress had some cigarette ashes on it, and J.L. pretended he was just brushing them off. Louise laughed.

She didn't laugh for long.

A chauffeured limousine, black and ominous-looking with tinted windows, was sitting on the tarmac as they pulled up. Neither Louise nor J.L could see anyone inside. Louise had remarked, "Must be a big celebrity flying in tonight."

As the two were sliding deeper into sexual pleasure, a slight figure in a fur coat slipped silently through the open hangar door. The figure of the shadowy brunette approached the car.

The first bullets from the gun were fired just as J.L. noticed this intruder. A fleeting look of horror crossed J.L.'s face as he realized that the dark figure with the small pistol was his wife, Cynthia. Louise never saw the other woman at all.

Shots rang out and the lovers lay dead in the black convertible, Louise with a red bloodstain rapidly spreading across the front of her white dress. Apparently as soon as Cynthia was sure that her husband and his mistress were dead, she put the small gun to her own right temple and fired. She slumped to the floor of the hangar, the final victim of the Tradewinds Triangle, the name the dead threesome were given in the press.

Since that double murder and suicide eighty-three years ago, visitors to the Tradewinds Airport report seeing a mysterious black limousine speeding away. Some say they see lights in unoccupied airport hangars, especially Hangar Number Twelve. There are voices that seem to be laughing in conversation in that hangar, even though no one is there. A woman wearing a white dress with a red stain on the bodice has been seen smoking a cigarette. She seems translucent. And a faint smell of Chanel perfume always drifts from Hangar Number Twelve.

## Background of the Cadillac Ranch: Amarillo, Texas

Just along eastbound I40 in a cow pasture, between exits sixty and sixty-two, you'll see ten Cadillacs, buried in separate eight-foot holes, nose down.

The Cadillac Ranch, as it is known, was the brainchild of a group known as The Ant Farm, three artists who worked together in a San Francisco studio until it burned down in 1978.

The three were Chip Lord (1944 - ), a professor of art at the University of California in Santa Cruz, Doug Michels, (1949-2003), who co-founded the Ant Farm in 1968 and won three *Progressive Architecture* design awards, and Hudsen B. Marquez (1947 -), who was the third member of the group that wanted to make a statement about the Golden Age of American automobiles, from 1949 – 1963. Encouraged by helium millionaire Stanley Marsh III, the three teamed up to half-bury ten Cadillacs of various vintages, nose down, at the same angle as the Great Pyramid of Giza.

The cars not only represent the "Fin years" of the American automobile, they embody the idea of mobility and the fascination with the freedom of the road that the American auto represented, especially with regards to Route 66.

The cars buried cost the artists anywhere from $700 (for the oldest, a 1949 Cadillac Club Coupe) to an average of $200 apiece and, when buried, their fins were forty-two inches off the ground. They represented the following years in automotive history: 1949 Cadillac Club Coupe (The artists said, "It ran so well, we hated to put it down."); 1950 Cadillac Series 62 Sedan; 1954 Cadillac Coupe de Ville; 1956 Cadillac Series 62 Sedan; 1957 Cadillac Sedan; 1958 Cadillac Sedan; 1959 Cadillac Coupe; 1960 Cadillac Sedan (flat top); 1962 Cadillac 4-window Sedan; and a 1963 Cadillac Sedan.

The entire ten cars had to be moved two miles west in August of 1997 but the original installation was complete on or about May 28th of 1974.

Later copycat projects include Carhenge in Alliance, Nebraska and Cars-on-a-Spike, in Berwyn, Illinois.

The following story circulates concerning the Cadillac Ranch, which encourages visitors to bring spray paint and paint the fins with fresh graffiti.

**Recent graffiti on a car at the Cadillac Ranch.**

## Cadillac Crazy

The young Indian boy opened the door to the field cautiously. Outside the fence, to his left, sat a box that looked like a large storage bin for tools. It was covered with graffiti and there were cans of spray paint lying nearby.

He had seen the sign, stuck in a yard, that advertised, "rooms to rent" at the Bates Motel.

Shower and taxidermy were mentioned on the hand-lettered sign stuck in a field across the frontage road from the entrance to the Cadillac Ranch, and, while Jose had smiled at the reference to the movie "Psycho," the lonely wheat field with the dust blowing directly into his face was less than inviting.

It was nearly dark, just as he had planned it. He clutched a can of red spray paint in one hand and a bottle of cheap champagne in the other. Tucked in the waistband of his jeans was a small plastic bouquet of flowers.

"It's such a shame that those cars were buried there when they were still able to run," Jose had told his friend John, who had chickened out on accompanying him on this trip. It's one thing if the car is already junk and doesn't run, but to drive a car to an early grave---especially a car as fine as a Cadillac. It's a crime, man! I feel for those cars."

John just gave him a look from between narrowed eyes. His friend Jose was one-of-a-kind. Only Jose would feel the need to slip out to the deserted wheat field to "christen" (as he put it) the tenth anniversary of the Cadillacs buried there on this May night in 1984 and to leave flowers at the cars' gravesite. The spray paint had been brought so that Jose could take part in the national pastime of leaving messages and designs on the abandoned autos.

"You're just crazy for Cadillacs, Jose," his friend said. "You've always had a soft spot for Caddies."

"Doesn't everyone?" asked Jose. "The Caddie is the classic luxury America automobile. Remember: it has the most powerful engine built in North America. The North Star engine. If you ever get to the point where you can afford a Cadillac, you've made it. You're on Easy Street. You're somebody."

John just laughed. "You're somebody, all right, Jose. You're somebody who's crazy for Cadillacs and probably deeply in debt."

This was true. Jose couldn't argue that point with John. He had always loved the look of the big American car. It was a sweet ride. There were other autos that had come along and tried to challenge the Cadillac's claim to being the sweetest ride in America, but, to Jose's way of thinking, none of them had succeeded. There had been some Chryslers whose fins had come close to rivaling the Caddie's for size, but the Chrysler, itself, was no match in ride and prestige.

"But why do you have to go out there tonight?" John asked. "There are some crazy people who stop by there to see those cars. You really ought to wait until it's broad daylight. It'll be spooky out there when the sun goes down."

John was probably right, but Jose wanted to memorialize the tenth year of the shrine's existence. It was 1984, just like the book title. To Jose, it all fit. He would go tonight, with or without his good friend John.

And so, here he was, all alone, pushing the wooden gate of the

field ajar.

The gate yielded easily. The walk to the cars was down a dusty, rutted, windswept lane, and he began the trip, casting looks from left to right as he went. John was right. It was spooky. It felt as though someone or something was watching him as he approached the buried automobiles.

First, Jose placed the small plastic bouquet next to the middle car in the ten-car line-up. Next, he walked to the far right end of the cars buried there and swung the champagne bottle with all his might, aiming at the round multi-colored wheel of one of the autos. When John had asked Jose about this plan, Jose had replied, "They christen ships that way, John. I think the $10^{th}$ year of the Cadillac Ranch ought to be christened in a special way, too."

The bottle would not shatter at first; the container of the champagne bottle was too sturdy. Jose placed his spray paint can on the ground, grabbed the bottle again with both hands, and swung as hard as he could, swung as though he were Babe Ruth swinging for the fences. The bottle's frothy contents bathed the brightly colored fin of the car that had finally punctured the container and Jose's hands got sticky as the champagne poured down the side of one of the autos.

Now for his message. Jose reached for the bottle of red spray paint, there on the ground near his feet, and, as he did so, the feeling, again, of being watched, intensified.

Just as he was starting to paint "R.I.P." on the side of the first of the beautiful, stately junked Cadillacs, someone (or something) grabbed him from behind, pinioning his arms.

He heard a man's voice say, "What do you think you're doing to these cars? You don't belong here. Leave the cars alone!"

The next thing he knew, there was a burlap bag over Jose's head, and he was being half-carried, half dragged towards some distant chicken coops.

Jose protested, "I'm not hurting anything, Mister. Let me go!"

He only got out the first two words before the mysterious stranger hit him with an object, knocking him unconscious.

When Jose awakened, there was a wrinkled old man crouched outside a chicken coop, staring at him, inside the coop. He began to realize that he had been struck in the head with his own can of red spray paint. Some of the can's contents had been released when he was struck, and now both his head and the man's clothing were stained with the red spray. The man looked like what John imagined an old prospector would look like: wizened, old, gray, hunched over. Yet he was surprisingly spry for someone who looked to be north of seventy, as he hunkered down outside the chicken coops and watched his young captive.

"Hey! Lemme' out!" Jose shouted.

The old prospector just smiled a toothless grin. And, for good measure, he grabbed the burlap bag that he had used in kidnapping Jose and wiped down the red-stained barrel of a small-caliber pistol he pulled from his waistband.

"Look.Mister…I don't know who you are, or what you want, but I just came to leave the flowers and paint the cars. I didn't mean no harm. What do you want from me?"

Still no answer from the old man.

Jose was shivering in the evening chill, now, and he wished, more than ever, that he had heeded his friend Jose's advice about visiting the Cadillac Ranch at sunset. It had seemed romantic, at the time, but now it just seemed foolish.

Finally, the old man spoke. "If you want to get out of here alive, you'll do as I say."

"Sure. Sure. Anything," said Jose. He nodded his head vigorously in assent, agreeing to the terms the old man might lay down.

" I need someone to see to these chickens, and I need to keep tourists like you from visiting after dark. It upsets the cars."

Jose recognized the sound of insanity when he heard it. He went with the program.

"Sure. Sure. Anything you say. Just let me out."

The old man gave him one last piercing look and asked a final question in a gravelly voice. "You won't try to run away, will you?"

"No. No," lied Jose. "I'll do anything you say." In his head, he was already measuring the distance from the chicken coops---which were approximately forty yards to the west of the cars---and, from there, to the fence and the gate. If he could reach the wooden fence at all, he was pretty sure he could climb over it, gate or no gate.

The old man began removing the metal pin that held the chicken coop door securely shut. The coop was about the size of a large desk. It smelled of chicken droppings, and Jose could not stand up inside it, so he was on his knees as the door slowly swung open. The old man still squatted there, watching him intently like a bird of prey.

Jose began to cautiously crawl through the open door. He didn't make any fast moves, initially. His head still hurt and his legs were cramped from being cooped up (no pun intended) for what seemed like hours. In fact, it might have been hours, as the sun had now sunk in the west, leaving only a large full moon to illuminate the dusty field.

The old man backed away from the door to the chicken coop as it swung open, and, in that moment, Jose leaped to his feet and began running for the fence, running for freedom, running as fast as he had ever run in his life.

He was thinking, the whole time, of an article he had read that said it was always better to try to run than to go with a would-be attacker.

That would have been true, except that the eccentric old man was a deadeye shot. Just as Jose reached the fence and began to clamber over it, the shots rang out and Jose fell backwards onto the dirt and pebbles of the field.

Jose heard the old man mumbling to himself as he lay there, mortally wounded, and the old geezer approached.

"I told you not to run. I warned you not to run. This is all your fault."

*******************************************

Those driving by on the I40 subroad saw a backhoe at the Cadillac Ranch site at dawn the day after Jose's visit. Those who saw it wondered if an eleventh auto was to be added to the line of ten classic cars. It dug a hole. It left. Nobody watched what went into the hole.

Jose was never seen or heard from again.

There have been reports that, in red spray paint, the name "Jose" and "John, help me!" is found spray painted on the cars. It happens on every anniversary of the Cadillac Ranch. Plastic flowers and empty champagne bottles are found then, also. But, despite his friend John's attempts to find his missing friend, no one ever saw or heard from Jose again.

**Rest in Peace**

**New Mexico: Land of Enchantment**

As we drive from the Texas Panhandle into New Mexico, just a short way along Route 66 is Tucumcari, famous for the slogan "Tucumcari Tonight."

Tucumcari was founded in 1901 and had a population of 6,194 at that time. In the 2000 census, the population was listed as 5,989. It lies near a flat-topped mesa to the south, which was a well-known Comanche lookout.

In the 1950s, Tucumcari became known as "the town of 2000 motel rooms", but, sadly, that is no longer true. The Blue Swallow Motel, however, founded in 1939 and famous for its blue neon sign still remains. So do Route 66 sculptures and a teepee shaped store. In its early days, the Chicago, Rock Island and Pacific Railroad ran through Tucumcari. It was such a rough town that it was dubbed "Six Shooter Siding."

The great Geronimo is credited with handing down this tale of the star-crossed Apache lovers Tocom and Kari, for whom the town is named.

The tragedy played out on a mesa that once served as an Apache lookout point.

As a halfway point on Route 66, the phrase "Tucumcari Tonight was an oft-repeated refrain of the Mother Road.

The following American Indian legend offers an explanation for the origin of the name from America's frontier days. The story could just as easily have been penned by William Shakespeare.

"Tucumcari Tonight" became a slogan for those traveling the Mother Road heading west. It was a sort of "halfway point," and its numerous motels (over 200 at one point), including the famous Blue Swallow, made it a travel destination.

## The Tale of Tocom, Kari and Tonopah

Apache Chief Wautonomah was growing old.

"My daughter," said Wautonomah to his beautiful daughter Kari, "you must soon marry a brave, so that I may see my grandchildren before I die."

"Father," said Kari, "you aren't going to die. You will live forever. Why do you constantly say these things? The Great Spirit will not let a chief as great as you leave his service on earth."

But Wautonomah was nearing the end of his earthly days. His bones felt the cold as they had not felt it in his youth. His eyes were no longer as keen, his aim with the bow no longer as sharp.

There were two braves who were the leaders of the young men: Tocom, who was fair of face and beloved by Kari, and Tonopah, who was equally brave, but with a disposition that caused many to mutter behind his back.

Kari and Tocom had been playmates and friends for all of their days; Kari had eyes for no one but Tocom. His dark shiny black hair captivated her and his glistening eyes entranced her. She could not tell her father of this, for the women of the tribe were chattel, to be given as brides to the bravest warriors.

And so it happened that Chief Wautonomah called both the young men of his tribe to his side and told them, "I will not live much longer. Soon, I will go to join the Great Spirit. One of you must take my place as Chief. Tonight, you must take your long knives and meet in mortal combat to settle the matter of who will be chief after my death. Whoever wins this fight will not only be the new leader of our people, but will have the hand of my daughter Kari to be his squaw."

Kari was by far the prettiest of the girls in the small village of teepees. She was known to have a lovely singing voice and cooked and cleaned and danced better than any of the other girls of the tribe. Plus, she was the Great Chief's daughter, so she was a prize to be treasured.

When the sun sank below the mesa, the two braves met on a flat place, bordered by trees and brush to the south. Unbeknownst to them, the fair Kari hid herself behind a large tree and watched the fight apprehensively, fearing for her lover Tocom.

First, it seemed as though Tocom was winning. His moccasins were swift as he struggled for position, but, alas, his foot slipped and Tonopah quickly seized the opportunity presented by his opponent's off-balance slip to plunge his long knife deep into the chest of the young brave.

Tocom fell to his knees, clutching his chest, while Tonopah stood behind him, watching warily to make sure that it was not a ruse.

When Kari saw the man she loved, Tocom, fall, mortally wounded and coughing up blood, she could not help herself. She rushed from the nearby brush where she had secreted herself, grabbed the long knife, pulled it from Tocom's chest and slashed the throat of the victor, Tonopah. Tonopah was taken by surprise and grabbed at the wound in his throat, all the while staring at the tiny Kari. She was so swift and decisive in her movements, that, before he could comprehend what was happening he was mortally wounded, his carotid artery severed by a slash of the small girl's hand. She had cleaned many guinea fowl and dressed many deer in the village. She knew what she was doing, even if she was not a warrior.

Kari then plunged the deadly knife that had now killed two of the finest young people of the tribe into her own chest and fell to the ground, mortally wounded, clutching her lover Tocom's hand. She lay her head on his chest for the last time, uttering the words, in Apache, "I do this for you, Tocom. You are my love. You are my life. Without you, I do not wish to live." She lay dead on the ground, her head resting on the bloody chest of Tocom. His rival, Tonopah, also lay dead nearby in a pool of his own blood.

The sounds of struggle alerted the tribesmen and Kari's father, Chief Wautonomah, came forth to see who had won the mano-a-mano battle between the two finest braves of the tribe. He was completely shocked to see not one but three bodies, and his own lovely daughter Kari among them.

"What have I done!" cried the anguished Chief. He pulled at his braids in horror, as he fell to his knees by his daughter's body.

Upon seeing what his poor advice had caused, Wautonomah grabbed the deadly long knife and thrust it deep into his chest, deep past his ribs into his aching broken heart.

As Chief Wautonomah fell, mortally wounded, he murmured the names of the two young people lying there together…"Tocom…Kari" before he breathed his last, his eyes settling into a glazed expression of eternal grief.

It was from the Great Chief's final words that the town received its name, some say, although others claim the town's name came from an Apache word meaning "to lie in wait."

If so, that name also applied to the beautiful but doomed Kari, who lay in wait until she saw her lover fatally wounded. Then, she rushed forth to avenge his death and take her own life.

There are those who say that when the wind rises high on the mesa, they hear the whispered sound of, "Tocom...Kari" in an ancient tongue.

Those who believe in this tragic story, a story surely sadder even than "Romeo and Juliet," believe in it, and also believe that the legend of Tocom and Kari was the source of the town's name. It is a refrain that drifts through the woods when the wind is blowing through the trees on the mesa.

***GHOSTS OF INTERSTATE 90*** Chicago to Boston  by D. Latham

*GHOSTS of the Whitewater Valley* by Chuck Grimes

**GHOSTS of Interstate 74**           by B. Carlson

GHOSTS of the Ohio Lakeshore Counties   by Karen Waltemire

*GHOSTS of Interstate 65*        by Joanna Foreman

**GHOSTS of Interstate 25** by Bruce Carlson

**GHOSTS of the Smoky Mountains** by Larry Hillhouse

GHOSTS of the Illinois Canal System by David Youngquist

*GHOSTS of the Niagara River*  by Bruce Carlson

**Ghosts of Little Bavaria**         by Kishe Wallace

Shown above (at 85% of actual size) are the spines of other Quixote Press books of ghost stories. These are available at the retailer from whom this book was procured, or from our office at 1-800-571-2665 cost is $9.95 + $3.50 S/H.

| | |
|---|---|
| Ghosts of Interstate 75 | by Bruce Carlson |
| *Ghosts of Lake Michigan* | by Ophelia Julien |
| **Ghosts of I-10** | by C. J. Mouser |
| ***GHOSTS OF INTERSTATE 55*** | by Bruce Carlson |
| Ghosts of US - 13, Wisconsin Dells to Superior | by Bruce Carlson |
| **Ghosts of I-80** | David youngquist |
| *Ghosts of Interstate 95* | by Bruce Carlson |
| Ghosts of US 550 | by Richard DeVore |
| *Ghosts of Erie Canal* | by Tony Gerst |
| Ghosts of the Ohio River | by Bruce Carlson |
| **Ghosts of Warren County** | by Various Writers |
| Ghosts of I-71 Louisville, KY to Cleveland, OH | by Bruce Carlson |

- Ghosts of Ohio's Lake Erie shores & Islands Vacationland  by B. Carlson
- Ghosts of Des Moines County    by Bruce Carlson
- Ghosts of the Wabash River   by Bruce Carlson
- Ghosts of Michigan's US 127    by Bruce Carlson
- **GHOSTS OF I-79**        **BY BRUCE CARLSON**
- *Ghosts of US-66 from Ft. Smith to Flagstaff*    by Connie Wilson
- **Ghosts of US 6 in Pennslyvania    by Bruce Carlson**
- Ghosts of the Lower Missouri        by Marcia Schwartz
- Ghosts of the Tennessee River in Tennessee    by Bruce Carlson
- **Ghosts of the Tennessee River in Alabama**
- **Ghosts of Michigan's US 12** by R. Rademacher & B. Carlson
- Ghosts of the Upper Savannah River from Augusta to Lake Hartwell   by Bruce Carlson
- **Mysteries of the Lake of the Ozarks**    Hean & Sugar Hardin

| |
|---|
| *GHOSTS OF DALLAS COUNTY*     by Lori Pielak |
| **Ghosts of US - 66 from Chicgo to Oklahoma**     By McCarty & Wilson |
| Ghosts of the Appalachian Trail     by Dr. Tirstan Perry |
| **Ghosts of I-70**     by B. Carlson |
| Ghosts of the Thousand Islands     by Larry Hillhouse |
| *Ghosts of US - 23 in Michigan*     by B. Carlson |
| **Ghosts of Lake Superior**     by Enid Cleaves |
| *GHOSTS OF THE IOWA GREAT LAKES*     by Bruce Carlson |
| *Ghosts of the Amana Colonies*     by Lori Erickson |
| **Ghosts of Lee County, Iowa**     by Bruce Carlson |
| The Best of the Mississippi River Ghosts     by Bruce Carlson |
| **Ghosts of Polk County Iowa**     by Tom Welch |

**GHOSTS of Lookout Mountain** by Larry Hillhouse

*GHOSTS of Interstate 77* by Bruce Carlson

**GHOSTS of Interstate 94** by B. Carlson

**GHOSTS of MICHIGAN'S U. P.** by Chris Shanley-Dillman

GHOSTS of the FOX RIVER VALLEY by D. Latham

GHOSTS ALONG I-35 by B. Carlson

**Ghostly Tales of Lake Huron** **by Roger H. Meyer**

Ghost Stories by Kids, for Kids by some really great fifth graders

Ghosts of Door County Wisconsin by Geri Rider

Ghosts of the Ozarks B Carlson

**Ghosts of US - 63** by Bruce Carlson

Ghostly Tales of Lake Erie by Jo Lela Pope Kimber

## To Order Copies

Please send me _____ copies of *Ghosts of Route 66 (Arkansas to Arizona)* at $9.95 each plus $3.00 S/H. (Make checks payable to Quixote Press.)

Name _____

Street _____

City _____ State _____ Zip _____

**QUIXOTE PRESS**
**3544 Blakslee Street**
**Wever IA 52658**
**1-800-571-2665**

---

## To Order Copies

Please send me _____ copies of *Ghosts of Route 66 (Arkansas to Arizona)* at $9.95 each plus $3.00 S/H. (Make checks payable to Quixote Press.)

Name _____

Street _____

City _____ State _____ Zip _____

**QUIXOTE PRESS**
**3544 Blakslee Street**
**Wever IA 52658**
**1-800-571-2665**